HAPPY BIRTHDAY, CUPCAKE!

Terry Border

PHILOMEL BOOKS An Imprint of Penguin Group (USA)

PHILOMEL BOOKS

Published by the Penguin Group | Penguin Group (USA) LLC
375 Hudson Street, New York, NY 10014

USA | Canada | UK | Ireland | Australia | New Zealand | India | South Africa | China
penguin.com | A Penguin Random House Company

Library of Congress Cataloging-in-Publication Data
Border, Terry, 1965–   Happy birthday, Cupcake! / Terry Border.   pages cm   Summary: On her birthday, Cupcake and her friend Muffin try to come up with an idea for a party that all of their friends, from Soup to Ice Cream Sundae, could enjoy.   [1. Birthdays—Fiction. 2. Parties—Fiction. 3. Friendship—Fiction. 4. Food—Fiction.] I. Title.   PZ7.B64832Hap 2015   [E]—dc23   2014022908
Manufactured in China by South China Printing Co. Ltd.   ISBN 978-0-399-17160-4
10 9 8 7 6 5 4 3 2 1
Edited by Jill Santopolo.   Design by Semadar Megged.   Text set in 21.5-point Hank BT.
The art was done by manipulating and photographing three-dimensional objects.

This book is dedicated to all the
makers of delicious cupcakes.
And muffins too.

"Today's my birthday," Cupcake said, "and I want to share it with friends! But what kind of party should I have?"

She called Muffin over to plan, and they took a long walk.

"I know!" Cupcake said. "I'll have a beach party! We'll make sprinkle castles and play in the sun."

"That *might* work," said Muffin, "but the beach
is so hot, and some of us might get drippy."

Cupcake touched her frosting. Muffin was right.

ROOT BEER FLOAT

"I know!" Cupcake said.
"I could get a big boat.
Who wouldn't come to
a floating party?"

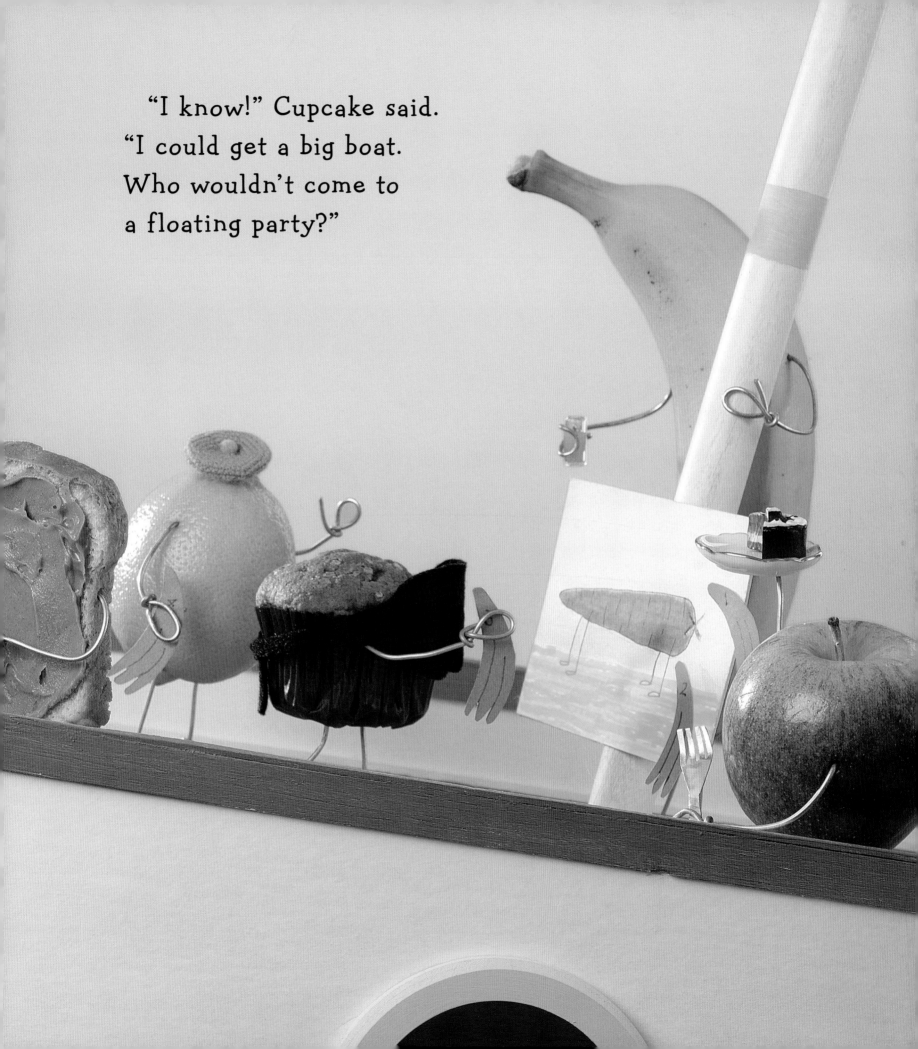

"That *might* work," said Muffin, "but if the ship rocks, Soup might lose his lunch."

Cupcake fidgeted with her wrapper. Muffin was right. She had to think of something else.

"I know!" Cupcake said. "I'll get everyone makeovers! It's so much fun getting frosted and sprinkled."

"That *might* work," said Muffin, "but I think *some* of your friends would find makeovers icky. Just think about Hamburger."

Cupcake felt like she was starting to crumble. Muffin was right again. Hamburger barely even liked himself with ketchup.

"I know!" Cupcake said.
"We could play musical
chairs! I could find a band!"

"That *might* work," said Muffin, "but if someone sits down really fast, you'll be squished!"

Cupcake didn't know what to do!
She was running out of ideas.
"Well, what about limbo?" she
asked. "With prizes for the winners?"

"Big prizes?" asked Muffin.
"Oh yes, that might work.
But can *you* get low?"

As they reached Muffin's place, Cupcake sighed.
"I'm going to go stale before I think of a good idea."
"Let's just take a break in my garden," Muffin said.
"That might work," Cupcake agreed.
Cupcake pushed open the gate and . . .

Cupcake's friends were all there!

And while they were dancing, a few friends did get a little drippy. Cupcake didn't limbo too well, and did get a little bit squished . . .

but it was still the best birthday party
that anyone could remember.